5-14-94

For Renee,

I hope you enjoy
reading this
all by yourself!

From your friend,

Janice Gibala-Broxholm

LET ME DO IT!

LET ME DO IT !

by Janice Gibala-Broxholm
illustrated by Diane Paterson

Bradbury Press   New York
Maxwell Macmillan Canada   Toronto
Maxwell Macmillan International
New York   Oxford   Singapore   Sydney

Bradbury Press
Macmillan Publishing Company
866 Third Avenue
New York, NY 10022

Maxwell Macmillan Canada, Inc.
1200 Eglinton Avenue East
Suite 200
Don Mills, Ontario M3C 3N1

Macmillan Publishing Company is part of the Maxwell Communication Group of
Companies.

First edition

Printed and bound in Singapore
10 9 8 7 6 5 4 3 2 1

The text of this book is set in Souvenir Regular.
The illustrations are rendered in watercolor.

LIBRARY OF CONGRESS CATALOGING-IN-PUBLICATION DATA
Gibala-Broxholm, Janice.
    Let me do it! / by Janice Gibala-Broxholm ; illustrated by Diane Paterson. —
1st ed.
        p.   cm.
    Summary: Four-year-old Katie seeks to prove her independence to her family
by trying to pour her milk, hold Grandma's yarn, and perform other tasks all by
herself.
    ISBN 0-02-735827-5
    [1. Self-reliance—Fiction.]   I. Paterson, Diane, date.   ill.   II. Title.
PZ7.G33909Le   1994
[E]—dc20   92-12856

For Scott,
my true love and inspiration
                    J.G.-B.

For Kaitlin Flavin...
who can do anything
                    D.P.

"Katie," her mom said, "where's your cereal bowl? Let me pour your milk." Katie looked at her mom and said...

"Let me do it!"

Katie's mom gave her the milk. But the carton was too heavy for Katie. The milk spilled all over the table.

Her mom gave her paper towels
and a sponge. Katie cleaned up the milk
all by herself.

After breakfast Katie went outside to wait for her mom. They were going to the grocery store. Her dad was washing the car. Katie looked at him and said...

"Let me do it!"

Katie's dad gave her the hose. When she squeezed the handle, the water sprayed *everywhere*. The trees were wet. The flowers were wet. Katie's dad was very wet.

Katie's dad laughed. He showed her how to turn off the water all by herself.

At the store Katie's mom told her, "We need a basket." When she reached for one Katie said…

"Let me do it!"

Katie pulled the top basket as hard as she could. All of the baskets fell around her.

Her mom picked up one basket for their groceries. Katie put back the other baskets all by herself.

When Katie got home, she ran to the
garage. She climbed onto her new bike.
Her brother said, "I'll help push you."
Katie looked at him and said…

"Let me do it!"

The bike started rolling down
the driveway. Katie tried to stop it.
She fell over and scraped her knee.

Katie's mom washed off her knee.
She gave her a bandage.

Katie put it on all by herself.

After supper Katie crawled onto the couch next to Grandma. She was making a sweater for Katie. When Grandma reached into her bag, Katie said…

"Let me do it!"

Grandma let Katie hold the yarn. When Katie stood up, it rolled off her lap. The yarn went under the table…

over the rug…

and it stopped next to the chair.
Katie chased the yarn across
the floor.

She rolled it back up all by herself.

That night after Katie brushed her teeth, she climbed into bed. Her mom had started to pull up the blanket, when Katie said...

Katie's mom let go of the blanket. She bent over and gave Katie a kiss. "I will let you do it," her mom whispered.

So Katie did it all by herself.